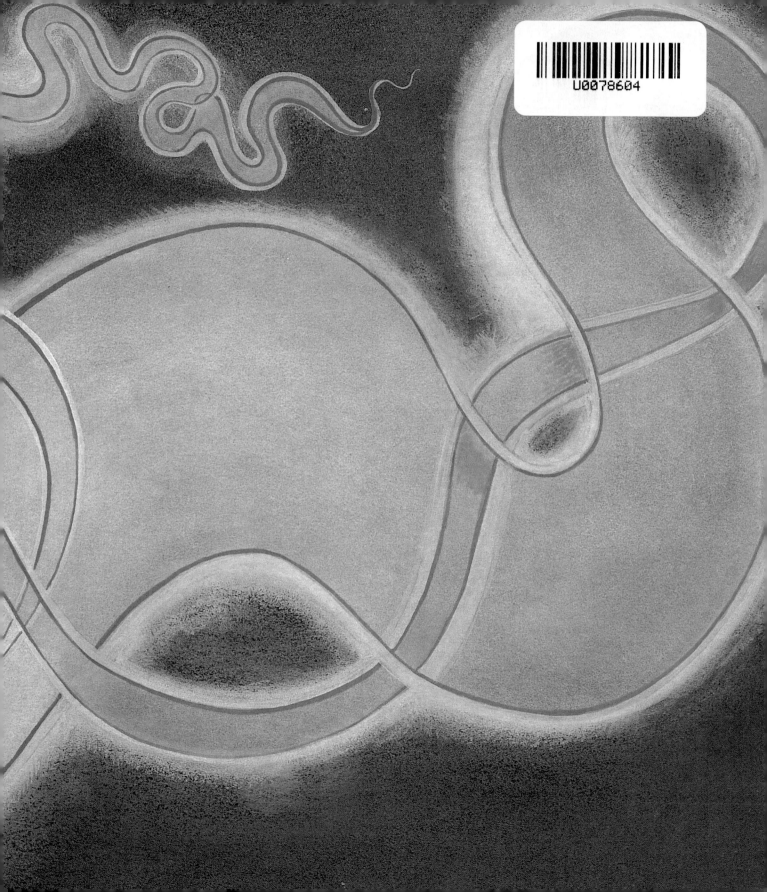

蒙弟闖幽靈屋

Gill Davies 著

Eric Kincaid 繪

洪敦信 譯

三民書局

Haunted House   ISBN 1 85854 775 X

Written by Gill Davies and illustrated by Eric Kincaid

First published in 1998

Under the title Haunted House

by Brimax Books Limited

4/5 Studlands Park Ind. Estate,

Newmarket, Suffolk, CB8 7AU

下雨天

The Rainy Day

Monty Mouse is bored. All his new friends are out or busy or asleep.
He has been **looking forward to** making a **den** in the garden between the plant pots, but it is raining very hard and he cannot go outside.
The other mice play games, **balancing** on a **cork**, but Monty is too upset to join in.

小老鼠蒙弟覺得很無聊。他所有的新朋友不是不在，或是正在忙，不然就是還在睡覺。他一直期盼著要在花園的盆栽中造一個窩，可是雨下得實在太大，他根本沒法兒出門！
其他的老鼠玩著在軟木塞上保持平衡的遊戲，可是蒙弟好煩喲！一點兒也不想加入他們。

"What about **calling on** Racer Rat?" suggests Ma Whiskers. "He might be lonely up there in the attic and would be glad to see you."

"What a good idea!" says Monty, cheering up. "I will do that right away." He scampers **straight** up the **stairs**. Half way up he meets Ghost.

"Can I come too?" asks Ghost.

"Of course," says Monty, and on they go together.

「去拜訪老鼠瑞瑟啊？」老鼠媽媽提議。「他在閣樓上可能蠻孤單的，看到你他會很高興的。」
「好棒的主意！」蒙弟高興了起來。「我立刻就去。」他蹦蹦跳跳地直接上樓去了。半路上，他遇見了幽靈。
「我也能去嗎？」幽靈問。
「當然可以啊！」蒙弟說，於是他們便一塊兒上樓去了。

They soon **reach** the attic. Racer Rat peeps out of a hole in the **ceiling** and **grins** at his friends.

"Hi there! Come on up," he cries. "It's nice of you to come and visit on such a rainy day."
The rain is **pounding** loudly on the attic **roof** as Ghost, carrying Monty, **oozes** up the ladder and through the hole.

reach [ritʃ]
勔 到達

ceiling [ˋsilɪŋ]
名 天花板

grin [grɪn]
勔 咧嘴微笑

pound [paʊnd]
勔 猛烈敲打

roof [ruf]
名 屋頂

ooze [uz]
勔 慢慢消失

不一會兒，他們就到了閣樓。老鼠瑞瑟從天花板洞口探頭出來了，對著他的朋友們開心地微笑著。
「嗨！上來吧！」他喊著。「你們真好，在這樣的雨天裡還來拜訪我。」
幽靈帶著蒙弟離開樓梯、穿過洞口，雨正乒乒乓乓地打在閣樓的屋頂上。

The attic is a lovely, **jumbly** sort of place that is full of boxes and books and pictures.

Legs the **Spider** sits on the **edge** of the **skylight**. He watches the world outside and the rain **pouring** down as the friends talk and laugh.

"Hey, everyone!" shouts Legs all of a sudden. "The rain has stopped."

jumbly [ˋdʒʌmblɪ]
形 亂糟糟的

spider [ˋspaɪdɚ]
名 蜘蛛

edge [ɛdʒ]
名 邊緣

skylight [ˋskaɪ͵laɪt]
名 天窗

pour [por]
動 傾注

閣樓是個既可愛又亂糟糟的地方，堆滿了箱子、書和圖畫。
蜘蛛長腿兒坐在天窗的邊邊上。這群朋友有說有笑，他在一旁瞧著外面的世界和不斷滴落的雨滴。
「嘿，大夥兒！」長腿兒突然叫了起來。「雨停了吧！」

"**A**t last!" say Racer
and Monty Mouse and
Ghost all together.
"**Yippee**!" shouts Monty.
"Now I can make my den."
They all say good-bye.
Then Ghost and Monty
fly downstairs. Monty has a lovely afternoon.
He makes a great den between the flower
pots. But **every now and then** he stops to
wave to Legs and Racer who are watching
him from the high attic window.

at last
終於，最後

yippee [`jɪpɪ]
㊟太棒了！好哇！

every now and then
時常

wave [wev]
㊟揮手

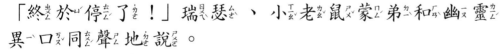

「終於停了！」瑞瑟、小老鼠蒙弟和幽靈
異口同聲地說。
「好耶！」蒙弟大叫說。「現在我可以去做
我的窩了。」
大家互道再見，然後幽靈和蒙弟就往樓
下飛奔而去。蒙弟度過一個美好的下午，
他在花盆間造了一個好大的窩。不過他
不時地停下來，向長腿兒和瑞瑟揮揮手，
他們一直在閣樓的窗邊看著呢！

媽媽驚魂記

Ma Has a Shock !

It is snowing.
When Monty
Mouse wakes up,
he is very **excited**
to see that the world
outside is all white.

As soon as they are **dressed**, all the mice
children rush outside to play. They **throw**
snowballs and slide and **build** a snow mouse
while Pa clears a path.
Suddenly they hear Ma **scream**.

excited [ɪk`saɪtɪd]
形 興奮的

dress [drɛs]
動 穿衣服

throw [θro]
動 投，扔

build [bɪld]
動 建造

scream [skrim]
動 尖叫

下ㄒㄧㄚˋ雪ㄒㄩㄝˇ了ㄌㄜ˙。
小ㄒㄧㄠˇ老ㄌㄠˇ鼠ㄕㄨˇ蒙ㄇㄥˊ弟ㄉㄧˋ醒ㄒㄧㄥˇ來ㄌㄞˊ，看ㄎㄢˋ到ㄉㄠˋ外ㄨㄞˋ面ㄇㄧㄢˋ一ㄧˋ片ㄆㄧㄢˋ雪ㄒㄩㄝˇ白ㄅㄞˊ的ㄉㄜ˙
世ㄕˋ界ㄐㄧㄝˋ，興ㄒㄧㄥ奮ㄈㄣˋ得ㄉㄜ˙不ㄅㄨˋ得ㄉㄜ˙了ㄌㄜ˙。
小ㄒㄧㄠˇ老ㄌㄠˇ鼠ㄕㄨˇ們ㄇㄣ˙一ㄧ穿ㄔㄨㄢ好ㄏㄠˇ衣ㄧ服ㄈㄨˊ，就ㄐㄧㄡˋ迫ㄆㄛˋ不ㄅㄨˋ及ㄐㄧˊ待ㄉㄞˋ地ㄉㄧˋ衝ㄔㄨㄥ
出ㄔㄨ去ㄑㄩˋ玩ㄨㄢˊ耍ㄕㄨㄚˇ。他ㄊㄚ們ㄇㄣ˙丟ㄉㄧㄡ著ㄓㄜ˙雪ㄒㄩㄝˇ球ㄑㄧㄡˊ、溜ㄌㄧㄡ冰ㄅㄧㄥ，還ㄏㄞˊ做ㄗㄨㄛˋ了ㄌㄜ˙
一ㄧ隻ㄓ雪ㄒㄩㄝˇ鼠ㄕㄨˇ，爸ㄅㄚˋ爸ㄅㄚ˙則ㄗㄜˊ在ㄗㄞˋ清ㄑㄧㄥ除ㄔㄨˊ小ㄒㄧㄠˇ徑ㄐㄧㄥˋ上ㄕㄤ˙的ㄉㄜ˙積ㄐㄧ雪ㄒㄩㄝˇ。
突ㄊㄨ然ㄖㄢˊ間ㄐㄧㄢ，他ㄊㄚ們ㄇㄣ˙聽ㄊㄧㄥ見ㄐㄧㄢˋ了ㄌㄜ˙媽ㄇㄚ媽ㄇㄚ˙的ㄉㄜ˙尖ㄐㄧㄢ叫ㄐㄧㄠˋ聲ㄕㄥ。

"Whatever is the matter?" cries Pa, rushing inside without **taking off** his boots.

There in the **porch** is Jim Fox, the **tramp**. He is fast asleep and **snoring** loudly. Ma Whiskers is **terrified** and is **shaking** all over.

All the animals from Hideaway House look **nervously** around the door.

take off
脫掉

porch [portʃ]
名 門廊

tramp [træmp]
名 流浪漢

snore [snor]
動 打鼾

terrify [ˋtɛrə‚faɪ]
動 使非常害怕

shake [ʃek]
動 顫抖

nervously [ˋnɝvəslɪ]
動 緊張地

「怎麼回事啊?」爸爸邊喊,靴子都沒脫地就衝進屋裡去。
流浪漢狐狸吉姆在門廊上。他正呼呼大睡,還發出好大的鼾聲。老鼠媽媽被嚇得全身發抖。
住在這棟躲藏小屋的動物緊張地圍在門邊觀看。

"If I know Jim Fox, he'll stay until Spring now," says Frog.
"Oh no!" cries Ma Whiskers starting to shake again.
"He can't! He just can't!"
Pa takes her out into the **dining room**, and all the animals **tiptoe** after them.
Meanwhile Ghost comes down to **find out** what is happening. He has heard Ma screaming.

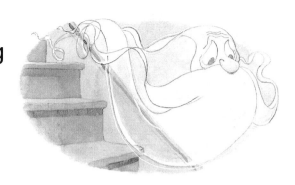

「如果沒錯的話，他會一直睡到春天的。」青蛙說。
「喔！不行呀！」老鼠媽媽大叫，又開始全身發抖。「他不能待在這兒呀！他就是不能待在這兒！」
爸爸把她帶到飯廳裡去，一夥動物也躡手躡腳地跟在他們後面。
就在這個時候，幽靈也下來看看究竟發生了什麼事，他也有聽到媽媽的尖叫聲。

host hopes Ma
is all right. He has
grown very fond
of Ma Whiskers —
and her apple pie.
"What is the matter?"
he asks. Monty **explains** and then **adds**,
"Foxes always **mean** trouble and Ma's
terrified of them."
"I know!" says Ghost. "Why don't I haunt Jim
Fox and see if I can **frighten** him away."
"What a great idea!" says Monty.

grow [gro]
勔 逐漸變成

explain [ɪkˋsplen]
勔 說明

add [æd]
勔 補充說明

mean [min]
勔 表示

frighten [ˋfraɪtn̩]
勔 嚇走

幽靈希望她沒事。他越來越喜歡老鼠媽媽——還有她的蘋果派了。
「怎麼了？」他問。
蒙弟向他說明一切，然後加了一句：「狐狸總是會帶來麻煩，而且媽媽很怕他們！」
「我知道了！」幽靈說。「何不由我去嚇嚇狐狸吉姆，看看能不能把他嚇跑。」
「真是太棒的主意了！」蒙弟說。

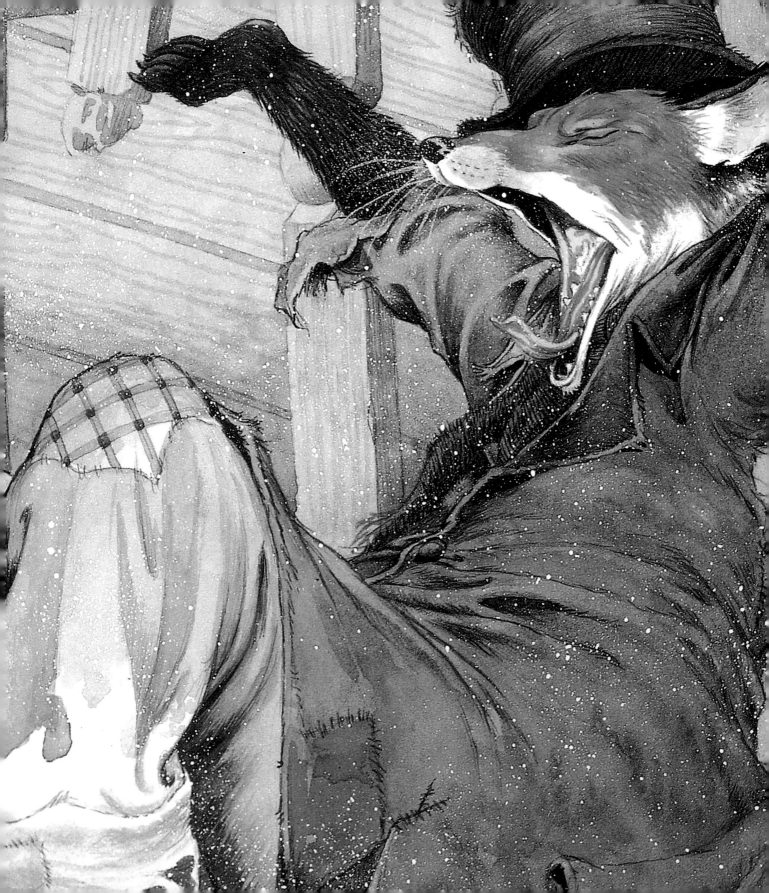

"Please help me," **begs** Ma Whiskers as Jim Fox **sneezes**, **yawns** and sits up to **scratch**.

Ghost practices swooshing and whoooing a few times. This is a **difficult** task for Ghost since his white shape **disappears** in the snow and the wind is howling louder than Ghost can. Finally Ghost is ready, but when he goes out on the porch, he finds that Jim Fox has gone back to sleep.

beg [bɛg]
動 乞求

sneeze [sniz]
動 打噴嚏

yawn [jɔn]
動 打呵欠

scratch [skrætʃ]
動 抓癢

difficult [ˋdɪfəˌkʌlt]
形 困難的

disappear [ˌdɪsəˋpɪr]
動 消失

狐狸吉姆一會兒打噴嚏、一會兒打呵欠，甚至坐直身子抓癢。老鼠媽媽乞求著說：「拜託幫幫我吧！」
幽靈練習了好幾次颼颼聲和呼呼聲。對他來說，這真是件不容易的差事啊！因為他的白色形體在雪中會看不見，風的呼嘯聲也比他的號叫聲還大！幽靈終於準備好了。不過，當他走到門廊時，他發現狐狸吉姆又進入夢鄉了。

23